Her Freeuse Escape

On Display and Public Fun

Lacey Cross

Paperback ISBN: 978-1-960162-35-9

CONTENTS

CHAPTER 1

I click through another webpage on my laptop while my husband Daniel's steady breathing beside me confirms he's asleep, unaware of my late-night research. I type "exclusive adult resorts" into the search bar, delete it, then try "freeuse vacation experiences" instead. There are so many more results than I expected.

What am I doing? I'm the woman who runs meetings with Fortune 500 executives without breaking a sweat, who plans vacations six months in advance with daily itineraries. Yet here I am, obsessively researching at 2 a.m. because I can't stop thinking about my friend Alyssa's recent trip.

My fingers tap methodically against the laptop case. Even in this private moment, I maintain my posture, shoulders back, the screen angled for optimal viewing. Always composed, always in control.

A webpage loads, displaying tasteful images of a Mediterranean-style resort. "Carnal Bay Retreat," the header reads in an elegant script. "An exclusive experience for discerning couples." My pulse quickens as I scan the carefully-worded description that manages to suggest everything while explicitly stating nothing.

Daniel shifts beside me. I quickly minimize the window and shut my laptop.

"Still working?" he mumbles.

"Just finishing up." I slide the laptop onto my nightstand and turn off the light before snuggling on my side next to him. "Go back to sleep."

"You've been distracted lately." His hand slides under my nightgown and curves over my stomach as he caresses my skin. "Something on your mind?"

My throat tightens. We've been married eight years, yet I can't bring myself to admit what I want in the bedroom. I don't usually ask for things—I'm the one who makes what I want happen. And I don't easily disclose insecurities or desires that might make me appear vulnerable.

"Just thinking about vacation options," I say, giving him a half-truth.

"Hmm." His hand slides higher, resting just beneath my breast. "Any particular destination?"

Now. Say it now.

"Actually..." I pause and almost chicken out. What is my problem? This is my damn husband. I should be able to say these things to him. "I've been looking into resorts. Like the one Alyssa visited."

In the darkness, I can't read his expression, and I get a moment of panic. Oh shit, I've miscalculated. I open my mouth to backtrack—

"The sex place?" His voice holds no judgment, just curiosity.

I consider denying it, but stop myself. "Yes. The freeuse resort."

Daniel props himself up on one elbow, now very awake. "Tell me more."

"You're not shocked?" I switch the lamp on, needing to see his face.

He laughs. "Mandy, I know you. You've been different since Alyssa told you about her trip. You've asked her for details three separate times. You've been distracted during sex." He tucks a strand of my hair behind my ear. "I figured you were either interested, or planning to start writing erotica."

"As if I have time to write...."

"So you're interested." His statement requires no confirmation.

I study the sheets as if they're the most fascinating thing in the world. "I found one in Florida. Carnal Bay Retreat. It's part of a collection of resorts that have freeuse days. Very exclusive." I'm retreating to my comfort zone of facts and logistics.

Daniel lifts my chin, forcing me to meet his gaze. "But why? You've never mentioned wanting something like this before."

The question strikes at the heart of what I've been avoiding. "When Alyssa described it—being free to just experience without planning, without being in charge—" I stop, frustrated by my inability to articulate my longing. "Everyone sees me as this competent person who has everything under control. Sometimes I want to just...not be that person."

Daniel's eyes darken. "You want to surrender."

The word 'surrender' makes me shiver. "Yes."

"To strangers?"

"Yes, but while you watch." My face flushes, and I wish I could bury my head into his chest while we have this conversation.

"While I watch," he repeats, his voice dropping an octave.

"Is that—would that be something you'd want?" I hate the uncertainty in my voice.

Daniel doesn't use words to answer. Instead he kisses me until I'm breathless and slides his hand beneath my night-shirt again to play with my nipple.

When he pulls back, lust is written all over his face. "I think the better question is: when can we go?"

Relief floods through me. I reach for him, but he catches my wrists, pinning them gently above my head with one hand. "Tell me more about this place."

"It's on a private peninsula that has a freeuse event for women once a month." I rock against him while I talk. My panties and his boxers are in the way, but I'm enjoying the pings of bliss as my pussy collides with his hardness. I'm already so wet, I could wrap my leg around him and he could slide in easily. "They have different colored wristbands that the women wear, depending on what they're consenting to."

"And what do you want men to do to you?" His lips brush my neck.

"I don't know yet."

"Yes, you do." He nips at my pulse point. "Tell me."

The words stick in my throat. Even here, with my husband, I struggle to voice my desires.

"I want—" I swallow hard. "I want to be used."

Daniel groans, "Keep talking."

"I want men to just take what they want without asking." The confession rushes out, and the words tumble over one another. "To use me without me having to decide or be in charge."

"And you want me to watch you turn into a little slut with these men?" He slides his hand between my legs and moves my panties aside.

"Yes," I gasp. "Just for the weekend."

"You're desperate to be a little fucktoy, aren't you?" He rumbles in my ear as his teeth graze my earlobe. "Say it again. Tell me what you want."

"I want to be used." A bolt of longing zings through me. "I want men to just bend me over and fuck me whenever they want."

Daniel sinks two fingers inside me, and I whimper as I rotate my hips to force his fingers in deeper.

"You're soaked." He pumps his fingers in and out. "You're such a dirty slut for me."

Holy shit, if he keeps up with this dirty talk, I'll bring up fucking other guys more often. He occasionally talks like this, but it's usually after a day of being turned on and he's had a beer to loosen his tongue.

He adds a third finger and my inner muscles clench around him. His thumb circles my clit and sparks dance along my nerve endings.

"Imagine it. Men lining up to fuck you. To fill every hole." He abandons playing with my clit to finger fuck me while his palm slaps my pussy with each thrust. "You're going to be a little fuckdoll for anyone who wants you."

My stomach quivers from delight and I moan, "Please."

He pins my wrists more firmly to the bed, and I squirm from the delicious feeling of being helpless.

But even in this moment, I have an internal director that choreographs my responses as pleasure builds. It's directing my every move like a photoshoot. I've spent my life choreographing every encounter.

Arch your back more. Moan a little louder. Bite your lip—he loves that.

"I'm going to watch them fuck you raw. Turn you into their toy until you're begging for their cum."

Ohhh, god. The thought of being filled by multiple men floods my mind, and my orgasm slams into me. Heat bursts low in my belly, spreading fast, and I cry out as the pleasure rushes through me, too big to hold back. For one perfect moment, my mind goes joyfully blank. This is the only time I ever stop thinking—when I come, and everything else just disappears.

Daniel continues to finger fuck me until the waves of euphoria fade. When he removes his hand from my pussy, he brings his fingers up to my face, painting my lips. I taste myself and moan as his cock probes my pussy.

"Is this what you want?" His voice is softer now. "You want to be my little slut that I share with whoever wants you?"

Mmm, hell yeah. I make sure my voice is clear. "I want that."

In response, he rolls over me, settling between my legs and bracing himself on one arm. He slams his cock deep, and I cry out in raw pleasure. My wrists are still pinned, leaving me helpless beneath him as he fucks me hard. God, I should've shared this fantasy years ago. Getting used by a bunch of men is right up there with my secret craving to be watched by strangers while I'm fucked—and this resort might just give me both.

"You feel so fucking good," he grunts as he chases his orgasm. I can tell he's not going to wait for me to come again.

I put my feet flat on the bed for better leverage as we frantically crash together. He releases my wrists so he can really hammer it home, and the wet, frantic rhythm of our bodies becomes a lewd symphony, spurring him on.

When his hand slides between us again and he fingers my clit, I'm lost. I get a few blissful moments where my brain turns off and my whole body shudders as I climax. The rapture skyrockets me to another plane and fireworks burst behind my eyelids. I cry out when I hit the peak, and Daniel groans as he unloads so much cum inside me, I'm not sure he's ever going to stop.

We ride out our orgasms together, and when we finally come down, he collapses next to me. The sheets are a tangled mess, and I can feel his cum dripping out of me. Mmm, that was wonderfully unexpected.

Daniel snuggles against me and kisses my neck. "Let's look into booking a vacation tomorrow."

I giggle, "I already bookmarked the information."

"Of course you did," he chuckles. "My sweet slut is always prepared."

Mmm, his sweet slut. I like this dirty side of him, and if I have to talk about taking multiple cocks more often to bring it out, I guess a girl's gotta do what a girl's gotta do.

Three days later, I'm in our home office, staring at the application forms on my computer. The questionnaire is far more detailed than I expected, filled with probing questions about sexual preferences, boundaries, and fantasies. I breezed through the logistical parts without hesitation, but now I'm stuck on the section labeled *Desires and Expectations.*

What do I even want? Other than men using me and dirty talk...

On impulse I call Alyssa and spill the tea about booking a trip. It all comes pouring out, and once I slow down, she giggles.

"I didn't know you wanted to be a freeuse slut. But are you sure you're ready for this? It's not exactly a controlled environment."

We've been friends since college, and she knows me better than anyone—except Daniel. "That's the point."

Alyssa is quiet for a moment. "You know, when I told you about my trip, I never expected you'd want the same thing. You were enthusiastic for me to try it, but you're so…"

"Uptight?" I supply.

"I was going to say 'measured.'" She laughs.

I think back to our conversations after her return—how I'd hounded her for details, how each revelation had triggered a rush of exhilaration that I'd carefully concealed.

"I can't get it out of my head," I admit.

"Daniel's on board?"

"Enthusiastically."

She pauses. "But seriously, Mandy, it's intense. You have to really let go."

"That's what I want." And it really is. I want to see if multiple orgasms from a bunch of men can make me stop analyzing everything to death.

"Well then, I hope you find so much pleasure your voice is hoarse from screaming."

Huh, how many times would I have to come for that? We chat some more and when we get off the phone, I focus on the questionnaire.

The cursor blinks at me. "Describe your ultimate fantasy scenario at a resort."

What exactly *is* my fantasy? I catch my reflection in the nearby mirror on the wall and automatically straighten up, brushing a hand over my hair as I offer myself a small, practiced smile. Always presentable, always polished—just the way I like it. Or is it?

Come on, just be honest. No one's going to judge you here. This is exactly why you're doing this.

I take a breath, let my shoulders relax ever so slightly, and turn back to the screen. *No holding back.* I begin to type.

CHAPTER 2

Daniel pulls into the circular drive of Carnal Bay Retreat and parks the car. My stomach twists as he reaches over and gives my knee a reassuring squeeze. "Well, we're here."

"We are." After several agonizing weeks of waiting, we've finally arrived.

A spark of excitement prickles beneath my skin. How long will it be before someone fucks me? I'm not wearing a wristband yet to signal I'm "open for business," so it won't happen the moment I step out of the car.

Stand up straight when you get out. Smile, but not too eagerly. Look confident but approachable.

The main building is made of white stucco with a terracotta roof and surrounded by large palm trees. It's simple, yet elegant, and the grounds are well maintained. I peer out the car window, trying to decide if it looks like a sex resort. It doesn't exactly scream "filthy things happen here," but since this is my first time visiting a place like this, I'm not sure what would say that.

A porter approaches, tanned and muscular, his biceps straining the sleeves of his polo. When his gaze settles on me, paired with a knowing smile, heat rushes to my cheeks. Is he one of the men allowed to use me? From the way my pussy clenches while my panties grow damp, I wouldn't mind if he was.

Wait—do they have designated men to service the guests? They must, right? All the employees can't be running around fucking people...otherwise, who would actually work?

Just smile at him—not your business smile, your seductive one.

I focus on grabbing my purse instead of gawking at him, but my fingers fumble and I nearly dump everything onto the car floor. I manage to catch it just in time, pulling myself together as the porter opens my door. So much for looking confident—but I still flash him a seductive smile.

"Welcome to Carnal Bay," he says, his focus lingering on me as I step out and straighten my linen dress.

I'm used to guys checking me out—I'm blonde and fit with generous breasts—but this is different. Usually, at work, the guys are covert about it, and no one openly leers. You don't want to mess with the woman in the power suit.

But knowing this guy might actually fuck me makes my skin tingle and my nipples tighten. My steps falter as we approach the entrance. One of my heels catches on the rockery path, and I stumble. I give a small yip of distress, and Daniel catches me before I fall.

"Whoa, you okay?" His eyebrows furrow in concern.

I'm usually graceful, but since I'm practically vibrating from pent-up lust, it's making me awkward. *Come on Mandy. You're not some bumbling intern. You're an executive who dominates at work.*

My grin is sheepish. "Yeah, just excited."

He winks in response, and a blush creeps up my neck. I wanted to not be in control, but this isn't exactly what I had in mind.

The main building's massive wooden doors swing open as we approach, and a second gorgeous male porter ushers us in. The cool air of the lobby is a relief from the humidity. The interior is elegant-casual with limestone floors, white-washed walls, and tropical arrangements. Again, nothing overtly sexual and I doubt a casual observer would think that I was checking in for a cock free-for-all....At least I hope I am. Just because I'm freeuse doesn't mean someone is going to use me.

I side-eye my husband. I mean, he's here so I'm guaranteed at least one cock. Oh man, that would be hilarious if we paid all this money and no one fucks me but him.

"Mr. and Mrs. Rivera." A woman glides toward us, hand extended, and I bring myself back to attention. "I'm Sophia, your hostess."

Her voice is pleasant and cultured. She's in her mid 50s with silver-streaked dark hair pulled into an elegant chignon. Her white dress clings to curves that put mine to shame. Is being drop-dead gorgeous a requirement for working here?

"Mandy," I say, taking her hand. "And this is Daniel."

Her smile encompasses us both. "Was your journey comfortable?"

"Very," Daniel answers. "The directions were great."

"Excellent." She gestures toward a seating area. "Please, let's sit for a moment before someone shows you to your villa. There are a few details to discuss."

We follow her to a cluster of plush chairs partially screened by tropical plants. A waiter materializes with a tray of beverages.

Sit with your knees bent, legs crossed at the ankles. Back straight but not stiff. Look engaged but relaxed.

"Our welcome tradition," Sophia explains, and Daniel and I each take a non-alcoholic beverage from the selection as Sophia raises her glass. "To new experiences."

I really could have gone with some liquid courage right about now, but Daniel and I made a pact to not drink on this trip. Neither of us want to hide behind the excuse that we were tipsy when we look back on the weekend.

After we all take a sip, Sophia sets her glass aside and produces a leather portfolio. "Now, as you know, today begins our monthly freeuse weekend for women." She extracts a glossy folder and hands it to me. "This contains our schedule of events, a map of the grounds, and your wristbands."

"Tomorrow night is our Roman Bacchanal," Sophia continues. "A favorite among our guests. Attendance is optional, but highly recommended. You can experience Carnal Bay's...atmosphere."

"Roman Bacchanal?" Daniel asks.

I explain. "A celebration inspired by ancient Roman traditions." My marketing brain fills in the details. "Feasting, wine, indulgence."

Sophia's smile widens. "Precisely. Though our version includes modern liberties. Togas are provided in your villa, though many guests choose to attend in varying states of undress."

From what little I know of Roman history, togas were worn by men and sometimes prostitutes. But since I'm not here for historical accuracy, I'm good with modern liberties. A toga seems like it will be easy to remove.

Sophia continues with the orientation. "The information in the folder explains everything, including our wristband system. Pink for vaginal consent, purple for anal, black for oral, and green for open consent to all forms. You can wear any combination that reflects your boundaries."

My throat tightens. Seeing the system laid out makes this very real.

"And the rules?" Daniel asks, his thumb tracing the lines on my palm.

"Simple," Sophia says. "Women wearing wristbands are available for the men here, all of whom have been thoroughly vetted. For everyone's safety, the men always move in pairs or small groups—like a built-in buddy system. And if anything feels off, the safeword 'red light' stops everything immediately."

I flip open the folder with trembling fingers. The black and pink bands peek out from the inside pocket–smooth silicone. Exactly the two colors I'd want to wear. I slip them onto my wrist, one after another, adjusting them so they're both visible. Daniel watches me, his lips curving upward.

Sophia turns to Daniel. "As her partner, you'll receive a tablet connected to our discreet camera system. You may watch from anywhere on the property."

"And privacy?" I manage to ask.

Keep your voice even. Don't let them hear the nervous excitement.

"There is none in the main areas," Sophia answers lightly. "The nature of the freeuse weekend is public enjoyment. However, your room remains private unless you choose otherwise."

She stands, signaling the end of our orientation. "The porter will bring your luggage and show you to Villa 12 now. It has an excellent view of the main courtyard."

The porter returns, joined by another man in the same uniform, and together they collect our bags. As we follow them through the main building, my gaze catches on a mirror mounted on the lobby wall. I take in my reflection—sexy but casual, just the look I was going for. If I were a guy, I'd definitely want to fuck me.

That's right. I look hot and ready. Own it.

Daniel glances at my wristbands, and anticipation coils tighter in my belly. I can't wait until we settle in—I'm already planning to suggest a walk around the grounds, hoping it leads to someone using me.

To distract myself from the growing heat between my legs, I joke with the guys carrying our luggage. "I don't think our two suitcases needed both of you. We didn't pack *that* much for the weekend."

The porter sets my bag down and turns to me, his expression shifting from professional to something more intimate. "They didn't need us both, but someone put her wristbands on already."

My heart rate speeds up. Oh, wow. I'm not even going to be able to unpack first?

Daniel's eyebrows rise, and he watches with interest as the porter turns me towards a side table and bends me over it.

Arch your back just enough. Look back over your shoulder—men love that.

The porter pins my shoulder down and I rest my cheek on the glass surface. His free hand is already sliding beneath my sundress. "This place really is everything we promise our guests."

I gasp as he fingers the lace of my panties. "Did you—are all staff part of the freeuse policy?" My voice catches as he pushes the fabric aside.

"Every one of us." He rubs my clit and my legs part instinctively.

"I didn't think—" My words dissolve into a sharp intake of breath as his fingers dip inside me.

"We provide excellent service. That's why guests choose this resort." The porter's voice drops lower. "To be available whenever, wherever, to whomever. That's why you're here right? To be used like a little slut."

A sudden surge of warmth courses through me as I picture a horde of men using me and calling me filthy things. I wrote down on the visitor questionnaire that I wanted dirty talk, but I didn't expect it before we got to our room. His fingers curl inside me, massaging a spot that makes my vision blur.

"Yes," I sigh, and close my eyes as he finger fucks me. Pleasure builds in my core, and my muscles tighten. This place already gets a five-star review from me.

When I hear laughter in the distance, my head whips up. "Hey, anyone could see us here."

The possibility sends an illicit thrill straight to my clit as I imagine people walking by, stopping to stare at me bent over.

"That's the point." His fingers continue to play with me, eliciting spikes of delight. I can't focus on anything but my impending orgasm. "You like knowing that anyone could walk past at any moment and see you bent over for a guy you don't know, don't you?"

Oh god, he's good. I'm unable to form words beyond a whimpered agreement of, "Yes."

His curled fingers repeatedly hit the pleasure point inside me. I buck into his hand, desperate for more.

"Say it," he demands as he brings his other hand between my legs to rub my clit. "Say you love it loud enough for your husband to hear you."

"I—I love it," I gasp and tense up as he brings me closer to the edge. I have no idea how I got to this point so fast, but I'll do anything to keep his fingers inside me. "I want people to see me like this and know that I'm a slut."

The porter chuckles, as if he's pleased. "That's right. And you'll be thinking about this moment all weekend, knowing you'd get on your knees and beg me to fuck you if I asked."

My mouth pops open in surprise and all I can do is moan as he increases the pace. He's right. I would gladly kneel before him if it got his cock inside me. I'm so close to coming, and my thigh muscles quiver as I wait for the euphoria to overtake me.

Just as I'm about to come, he stops. I whimper in protest, desperate for him to finally give me his cock. I glance back at him, and his fingers glisten as he brings them to his mouth.

He sucks them clean. "Tasty," he says with a satisfied smile. "Now, let's get you to your villa."

What? I look at Daniel in disbelief and I swear to God he's trying to hide a smile. What sort of fucked-up resort is this?

My husband helps me stand and straightens my clothes as if I'm helpless—which to be honest, I basically am right now. My body is about ready to riot without an orgasm. When Daniel's hand brushes across my nipples, the resulting ache earns him a glare. This time he can't hide the upturn at the corner of his mouth. Oh yeah, he's enjoying my pain. But underneath his amusement, I can tell he's turned on—and the bulge in his jeans confirms it.

Compose yourself. Fix your hair. Don't let them see how desperate you are.

The porter is professional now, all evidence of our encounter erased from his demeanor. The second one just stands back and watches, but when I peek at his slacks, there's a pronounced bulge. Before I can tease him and ask if he wants me to blow him, we start walking again.

As we follow the porter, I notice the strategic placement of benches in secluded alcoves. There's an abundance of surfaces at just the right height. They're making this easy for people to have sex in a variety of locations, and to be watched.

Villa 12 sits apart from the others. Our room is decorated with white linens and natural wood and a massive bed dominates the main room. There are sliding glass doors that open to a private terrace that overlooks the main courtyard. Sophia wasn't lying about the great view. If someone was having sex out there, we'd have front row tickets.

"Your welcome package is on the desk," the porter says, indicating a basket filled with snacks, fruit, and what appears to be lube. "Your tablet is charging by the bed—once you turn it on, it'll automatically connect with the observation app."

The idea of being on camera fills me with an intoxicating surge of adrenaline. Not just for Daniel's enjoyment, but potentially anyone with access to the system. I imagine strangers watching me get fucked and commenting on the show. I press my thighs together to ease the sudden ache.

The porters each give me a final smile before they leave, and I stay frozen in place until the door clicks closed behind them.

Once we're alone, I turn to face my husband. "You liked that, didn't you?"

"Which part? The part where you were bent over getting finger fucked, or the part where he didn't let you come?"

Oh yeah, he's in trouble. "Daniel—"

"I loved it." He wraps his arms around me. "Seeing someone else want what belongs to me—what I'm choosing to share."

I give him my best pout. "But I didn't get to come."

"How about this, baby?" He pauses to give me a spine-tingling kiss. Our tongues slide and tease each other, and I imagine forcing him onto the bed and riding him. Who needs the porter anyway? When he breaks off the kiss, I'm ready to shove him down, but his words stop me.

"How about for every orgasm you feel you didn't get this weekend, I'll make it up to you when we get home?"

Oh hey, what's this? I blink at him while my sex-crazed brain considers his offer. So I'll come as many times as I can on the trip, and then my husband is going to give me even more orgasms at a future date? I don't see how this is bad.

"Deal."

He looks like he's about to kiss me again, but instead he steps back. "Let's get some air."

He crosses to the terrace doors and opens them, letting in a warm breeze.

"Come look at this view," he calls.

Is he trying to deny himself? If I were him, I'd be banging me all over the villa by now. I join him outside. Below us, the main courtyard stretches out—multiple pools, cabanas, and lounging areas, all designed with clear sightlines. I imagine it filled with men who will see my wristband and simply take me.

"You're tense," Daniel says, stepping behind me and massaging my shoulders.

"You would be too if you were just left hanging."

"You don't have to participate," he reminds me. "Nothing happens unless you wear the wristband outside our room."

I turn in his arms. "I want this. I'm just..."

When I don't continue he finishes for me. "Scared of not having control?"

"Yeah," I nod, grateful he understands. "Let's look at the pamphlet."

Back inside, we sit on the bed and check out the information about the weekend. The schedule lists various activities tomorrow—naked morning yoga, brunch, pool games, and then the Roman Bacchanal.

Along with the information are the last two silicone wristbands—purple and green. I touch them lightly, imagining each one around my wrist.

"Are you going to keep the black and pink ones on?" Daniel asks, his voice carefully neutral.

I look up at him. "What would you want to see?"

"If it were my choice? Pink and black. Maybe green." He gives me a devilish smile. "I want to see you spit-roasted, but this is your decision."

I imagine being bent over while a stranger takes me from behind, and another man filling my mouth while Daniel watches.

"Yeah, pink and black," I repeat.

"For now," Daniel says. "You can always change your mind. Add the green later if you want."

I laugh lightly. "Let's not get ahead of ourselves."

He kisses me again, possessively, and his hand slides up my thigh beneath my dress. "We have a few hours before dinner," he murmurs against my lips. "How should we spend them?"

Okay, fuck waiting. I push on him and he falls backwards onto the bed. He sighs in pleasure as I straddle him. I have a sudden need to assert control while I still can. Later I'll surrender, but right now, I need to bounce on my husband's cock.

"I have some ideas," I tell him, reaching for his belt.

CHAPTER 3

After my first orgasm of the trip and an early dinner, I decide it's time to check out the pool area. Before I go, I slip on my white bikini and adjust the pink and black wristbands, making sure they're both clearly visible.

I pause by the mirror and take a long look at myself. *Not bad at all*. I straighten my shoulders, adjust my top for the most flattering fit, and let a sly smile curl my lips. If I saw me walking by, I'd definitely stare.

Blowing a kiss to Daniel, I grin. "See you soon!"

He's eager to watch everything unfold on the tablet, which is just fine by me. Knowing my husband, he's probably scoping out all the camera angles to catch as much action as possible. I'll have to make sure I give him a good show.

Shoulders back. Chin up. Walk with purpose, but not too much urgency.

Dusk is just settling in, and the pool glows under carefully placed lights, turning the water into liquid sapphire. I scan the area, noting sight lines and possible setups. The chairs are the perfect height for bending over, and the steps in the shallow end would give me excellent leverage for all kinds of positions.

Since it's dinner hour, the pool area is empty. So much for finding a bunch of men to fuck me. My carefully planned entrance wasted on an audience of none.

I kick my sandals off and settle onto a lounge, arranging my limbs in what I know is my most flattering pose—one leg slightly bent, arms posed to accentuate my cleavage. My mind is a jumble of concerns. What if no one approaches me all weekend? What if they do and I freeze up? What if I look ridiculous? I should have practiced more poses in the mirror before coming down.

Daniel really isn't getting much of a show from me, but I'm sure someone here is getting a good pounding on screen. The idea of other couples potentially watching guys fuck me from the privacy of their rooms makes me needy and impatient.

Fuck it, I'll go for a swim. At least I can give Daniel something to watch. Just as I sit on the edge of the pool and am about to lower myself into the water, two men approach from the path to the main building.

They're in their mid-thirties, fit, one with dark curly hair, the other with a close-cropped blonde style. They notice me—or more specifically, my wristbands—and exchange a look. My heart hammers and I swirl my feet in the water, pretending not to notice them while being acutely aware of their approach.

Look casual but inviting. Not too eager.

The blonde one is wearing swim trunks and an unbuttoned linen shirt. His friend is in blue board shorts with nothing on top. His chest has just the right amount of hair and I imagine running my fingers through it.

"Mind if we join you?" the blonde one asks, his voice carrying a slight Southern drawl.

"Go for it." I shrug with practiced nonchalance and the blonde one sits down next to me on the edge while the friend hangs back.

They introduce themselves—Tyler is the one who sat down and the brown-haired guy is Justin. We make casual conversation about the weather, and how long I'm staying. Normal chitchat that feels surreal given the context. I answer on autopilot, hyperaware of my body, and the way the water glistens on my legs. I'm performing already, calculating each response for maximum effect.

Am I supposed to be seductive, aloof, or just myself? Should I tell them they should just fuck me? It's not like I'm going to say no...

My skin flushes as I think about Daniel watching on the tablet. Will he be able to see my face when I come? Will he hear every moan, every gasp? But maybe the cameras don't have sound.

"First time at Carnal Bay?" Tyler asks, and I give a soft, playful laugh.

"Is it that obvious?"

The anticipation of what they're going to do—or more specifically how they're going to do it—has my bikini bottoms damp. I cross and uncross my legs, a deliberate movement designed to draw attention.

"Only a little." He touches my knee, and my clit throbs as he drags his gaze over me, heating me up from the inside out. I resist the urge to push my chest out to make my breasts look fuller.

"Did you come here with someone?"

I nod. "My husband. He's...watching." I tilt my head slightly, letting my hair cascade over one shoulder.

"Good. That's what makes this special, isn't it?" Justin finally comes to sit on my other side, effectively bracketing me between them. "Knowing he's seeing everything."

My breath catches, and I twine my fingers together in my lap so they can't see I'm trembling. I need to appear confident, in control, even as I'm supposedly surrendering it.

"You seem tense," Justin says and he leans in and kisses the side of my neck. "That defeats the whole purpose."

Maybe if they'd just fuck me, I'd be able to stop thinking and relax. The words catch in my throat—it feels strange, sharing something so personal to strangers—but I force them out anyway. "I'm just—I'm usually the one in charge. At work, at home. Everywhere."

Justin chuckles. "Well, you aren't here."

I immediately want to challenge him because I still feel very much in charge, but Tyler suggests, "Close your eyes." He kisses my neck and his breath is warm. "Don't think about us. Don't think about anyone else. Just feel."

I hesitate, then let my eyelids fall shut. I'm still directing myself—head tilted, lips slightly parted. Tyler continues to kiss my neck while Justin caresses my thigh, slowly moving higher towards my bikini.

"That's it," Justin croons. "No performance necessary."

Their touches stay light, exploratory, while my mind races in a thousand directions. Should I shift to a better angle for them? Am I supposed to be doing more? What do I look like on camera? Is my stomach flat enough like this?

"You're still thinking too much," Tyler observes. "I can practically hear the gears turning."

I laugh despite myself. "Sorry. I'm trying." I force my shoulders to relax, consciously unclenching my jaw. This isn't a board presentation. This is supposed to be surrender.

I sense Tyler's movement and I hear a splash. We're at the shallow end so the water would only be up to his waist. He hooks his fingers into my bikini bottoms and I shift from side to side so he can remove them. It takes extreme effort to not watch him as he parts my legs.

Knowing he's looking at my pussy makes something shift inside me. The constant internal narrator quiets slightly, but doesn't disappear.

"Beautiful." Tyler hums the word, and heat ripples through me as I spread my legs for him.

I moan when he explores the crease of my thigh and his fingers brush my pussy lips. Tyler slides a finger inside me and spreads my wetness to my clit. His strokes make me wiggle against his hand. Nothing is going as I expected, but I'm not complaining.

Justin runs his fingertips from my shoulder to the swell of my breast and my nipples harden, begging for his touch. He pulls my bikini top up and his thumb grazes my nipple. A zing of pleasure heads straight for my clit. Everything they're doing is like a delicious tease that makes me feel more alive.

When Justin tweaks my nipple almost painfully, I gasp. I'm so turned on, the world is a little hazy. He tugs on my other nipple and I bite my lip to hold back my moan. He's hurting me, but it's a pleasurable pain. I wonder if I should let myself be loud—Daniel would probably enjoy hearing me.

"I think..." Justin pauses to pull on my nipple again. "The slut is warmed up. What do you say?"

A surge of heat rushes through me. Oh yeah, I'm warmed up.

Tyler chuckles. "I think you're right." He slides his finger out of me, and I feel a pang of emptiness. But before I can process it, he pulls me into the water with him. The water is the perfect temperature, but it's still a contrast to my overheated skin.

Justin gets up and walks over to the stairs leading into the pool. He sits on one of the steps above the water and takes his cock out of his shorts. "Bring her over here. I want to use her mouth."

Oooh, here we go. Tyler picks me up bridal style and carries me over to Justin. When he sets me down, Justin spreads his legs and I crawl between them. He's high enough on the steps that I have to kneel on one of them. My legs are in the water, but my ass isn't.

I arrange myself carefully—back arched just enough, head at the optimal angle for both pleasure and visual appeal no matter where the cameras are located. Justin holds onto the base of his shaft as Tyler guides my head to it. I part my lips, eager to taste my first cock at the resort. The tip is already slick with pre-cum, and I open wider, taking him in.

My tongue swirls around his shaft, feeling every ridge, every vein. His pre-cum tastes different from Daniel's, which makes this feel dirtier. Daniel better be watching this. I'm being a slut, and I love it.

Tyler pulls my asscheeks apart and angles me so that I'm fully exposed to him. I moan around the cock in my mouth as I imagine he's about to fuck me from behind.

"You should see yourself," Tyler says. "On your knees, cock in your mouth—you're a natural fucktoy."

Knowing that I'm letting two guys I don't know use me makes my head spin, and I feel like this is what I was meant to do. I can't believe how much I'm enjoying this. He's right–I am a natural fucktoy and it's liberating.

Justin tangles his hands in my hair, guiding me up and down his cock. "Suck harder, slut. Give me the best blowjob of your life."

He fucks my mouth and I gag a little. He's not being overly forceful, but it's just enough to make me feel like he's controlling me and making me do what he wants. I don't want him to stop.

Tyler's fingers caress the curve of my ass, dipping between my legs. He finger fucks me with two fingers, stretching me open. "The slut is ready for my cock."

Justin tugs my head up and his cock pops out of my mouth. I gasp for breath, a string of saliva connecting my lips to his shaft. "Tell us what you are," he demands.

I hesitate, my mind racing. Tyler's fingers are still inside me, curling, hitting that spot that makes me writhe as the pressure increases. "I—I'm a slut." The words tumble out. "I'm a fucking slut!"

When Tyler thrusts particularly deep, my mind goes blank for three marvelous seconds.

Justin gives me a wicked grin as he strokes his cock. "That's right. And what do sluts do?"

"They—they fuck and suck."

Tyler finger fucks me faster and harder, and I moan.

"That's right...fuck and suck," Justin says. "And we're going to use your holes because you aren't even really a slut. You're just two holes waiting to be filled with cum."

Oh god, he's right. If there were more men here right now, I'd beg them to line up and use my holes however they wanted. Hell, if I was wearing the green wristband, I'd beg someone to fuck that hole too.

Tyler continues to pump his fingers in and out of my pussy as the rapture builds. I won't be able to hold back my release, and I don't intend to.

"Now say it again." Justin tightens my hair in his fist and pulls my head back, forcing me to look up at him. "Tell us what you are."

"I'm just two holes for cum," I gasp out, the admission making my pussy clench with desire.

Justin's grip tightens as he pushes my head back down to his cock. "Now do your job so I can blow my load down your pretty little throat."

I eagerly take him back into my mouth as Tyler removes his fingers from my pussy. The head of his cock nudges my entrance before he slams into me. I'm shoved forward onto Justin's cock and the bliss is so intense, I almost come right then. For a brief moment, my mind quiets again from the overwhelming sensation of being filled from both ends.

"Fuck, this hole is tight." Tyler drives into me and each thrust makes me tremble from joy.

Suddenly, I really am nothing but two holes as Justin grips my head, guiding me to match their rhythm while they take their pleasure from me.

"Such a good fucktoy," Justin groans, and I suck harder on his cock in response. Daniel better not be missing this, and I hope he's got his cock out. I imagine how we must look on camera—me sandwiched between two men.

"Fuck, I'm close," Tyler grunts, his thrusts growing rougher. He drives into me hard, his cock throbbing as he spills hot cum inside me, tipping me over the edge. Rapture crashes through me as I moan around Justin's cock, trembling with pleasure.

Justin holds my head still as he thrusts into my throat. "Swallow it all, slut," he commands, and his cock spasms as his cum coats my throat and tongue. I swallow as quickly so I don't lose a drop.

When they both pull out of me, I'm still trembling with aftershocks of pleasure. Justin scoops me up from the water, cradling me to his chest as he carries me to the lounge chair and eases me down gently. Tyler disappears for a moment before returning with bottled water.

He opens it for me and puts it in my hand. "Drink up. We won't leave you until we know you'll be okay."

I hold in a giggle and take a sip. When I rest back and close my eyes, the water bottle is removed from my hand. I'm floating in a haze of happiness when I hear the slap of leather on the pavement.

"Hi guys. I'm her husband. I'll take it from here."

My bikini top is still pulled up and my bottoms are by the edge of the pool. I'm wet, and I'm sure my hair is a mess. I crack an eye open and beam at Daniel. "Hi!"

He leans down and gives me a thorough kiss that makes my insides simmer. "Hi, my slut."

Yeah, he's definitely earning himself a reward today.

The guys say their goodbyes to us, and Justin winks at me before they both turn and head down the path. There's a lingering warmth in my cheeks and a neediness between my legs.

"Ready to go back to our room?" Daniel asks, and by his tone I can tell he's turned on. Oh yeah, he saw the entire thing.

I nod, still feeling a bit dazed. He helps me up and holds me steady as I put my bikini bottoms back on and adjust my top. He wraps a towel around me that he must have brought with him.

Once my sandals are on, I lean into him, inhaling his familiar, comforting scent. I just got spit-roasted by two guys, and now it feels like I'm home as Daniel slings his arm around my waist. As we walk, his thumb strokes my hip and my desire grows.

Back in the villa, Daniel takes me straight to the bed. He sits down, pulling me to stand between his legs. "Tell me what you felt."

Oh god, how do I even begin to explain it? "It was like I was completely out of control, and it was incredible."

It might have been brief, but those few moments when my mind finally went quiet...that was something else entirely.

His voice roughens with hunger. "And what are you now?"

"Oh..." I feel myself blushing. "You could hear us too?"

"I heard everything." His gaze is unyielding, coaxing the truth from me.

"I'm a slut. Your slut."

A slow smile spreads across his face. "That's right."

He slides his hands up to cup my breasts, and I moan as he plays with my nipples.

"And what does a slut need?" His voice is husky, and I arch into his touch.

"She needs to be fucked by her husband."

He chuckles. "That's right, my love. And I'm going to fuck you. But first..." He rises to his feet and turns me toward the bed.

When he bends me over, I brace my palms against the mattress to steady myself. He tugs my bikini bottoms down, baring my still-wet pussy.

"First..." He trails his fingers along my soaked folds. "I want to watch my cock slide into your well-used pussy. I want to see their cum dripping out of you as I fuck you."

Oh god, that's hot. I glance back at him and give my ass a teasing wiggle. After the experience I just had, the filthy words slip out easier than I ever imagined. "Then do it. Fuck your slut. Use me like the fucktoy I am."

He pulls his shorts down and when the tip of his cock nudges at my pussy, I face forward and just enjoy the moment. He rubs my clit with the head of his cock before sliding in. I moan loudly when he bottoms out, and I can tell I'm going to come quickly.

He leans over me, grabbing my swinging breasts and pulling at my nipples while he fucks me. I can feel wetness leaking out of me, and I imagine it's Tyler's cum as a surge of delight ripples through me.

"That's it," Daniel growls. "Take my cock like the good little slut you are."

I moan, the sound caught between a gasp and a cry as I come undone. For a glorious moment, my mind goes completely silent before I chant, "Fuck me, fuck me," as I slam back towards him, greedy for every moment of bliss.

"Fuuuuck, Mandy," He groans and explodes inside me. He spasms and jerks, mixing his cum with Tyler's.

When he's done, he withdraws and we collapse onto the bed into each other's arms.

"My good little slut," he says, his voice soft and sated.

If I had known he was going to fuck me a bunch this weekend, I would have been even more eager to get here. This is the best of both worlds. Is he going to keep going crazy after other guys use me? It's wonderful.

I smile as my eyes flutter closed. Yep, I am his slut. And this slut still has another day to try to find that elusive moment when my mind finally, completely shuts off. I drift off to sleep, eager for what tomorrow will bring.

CHAPTER 4

The next day, Daniel and I have breakfast in the dining room at the main building. He enjoyed watching so much last night that he wants to do it again today. After we eat, I slip away from the table, leaving Daniel chatting with another couple.

I have a plan. There are plenty of intriguing areas at the resort, but when I looked at the map this morning, something called 'The Secluded Grotto' caught my attention.

As I stroll through manicured gardens, I daydream about what someone could do to me in all the hidden alcoves on the property. The morning is warm and I'm wearing a sundress with no panties—easy access. My pink and black wristbands are clearly visible. I'm impatient. This is our last day and I need more cocks.

The path descends between two large boulders, and I hear the sound of trickling water before I see the source. The grotto opens up—a natural stone enclosure with a small waterfall feeding into a pool. Lounges surround the water, and discreet lighting illuminates the space despite the overhead canopy of trees.

I pause at the entrance. Three men occupy different spots around the pool. One is sprawled out on a chair reading—he's shirtless, his shorts riding low on narrow hips. Another floats lazily in the water. The third stands near the waterfall, adjusting something on the wall—a control panel of some kind.

They notice me simultaneously. The shift in energy is immediate—their casual postures tightening with interest, and they track my movements as I step fully into the grotto.

"Good morning," I say, hiding my anticipation behind my marketing executive voice. I'm a woman on a mission to get fucked, and hopefully these guys provide.

The man by the waterfall approaches first. He stands close enough that I catch his scent—clean, with hints of sandalwood.

"I'm Miguel." He gestures to the others. "That's Chris in the pool and Ben on the lounge."

I sound surprisingly breathy when I introduce myself. "I'm Mandy."

Miguel smiles and slides his hand down my back before moving lower to cup my ass. "The grotto has some interesting features. Would you like a tour?"

"I'd like that." I don't add what I'm really thinking: as long as it ends with a cock in me.

Miguel guides me toward the waterfall. "The water temperature is adjustable," he says, motioning to the control panel. Then he gestures to the curved alcoves carved into the wall, each one deep enough to fit multiple people, with cushions tucked inside. "These are designed for privacy...or for certain positions," he adds, his tone suggestive.

"The acoustics are great too," Chris adds, emerging from the pool. Water streams down his chest while his shorts cling to his powerful thighs. "Sounds don't carry beyond the grotto."

I notice small cameras around the space, and my clit throbs at the sight of them. Someone could be watching right now—Daniel, other guests, maybe even staff. The thought of being their entertainment, their live sex show, gives me a naughty thrill.

"This dress looks lovely," Miguel says as he fingers the thin straps on my shoulders. "But it's unnecessary."

He slides the straps down my arms and I remain still as he undresses me. The fabric pools at my feet, leaving me naked except for my sandals and the bands around my wrist.

"Beautiful from behind as well," Ben comments, approaching me.

Hands touch me from multiple directions—Miguel traces my collarbone with his fingers, while Ben palms my ass and Chris plays with my nipples. I stand still, fighting the urge to tell them where to touch me.

"Do you know how the resort makes sure you get what you want?" Miguel asks, his lips brushing my neck.

What? No—how would I know? My mind scrambles for an answer, but I come up empty. When I stay silent, he goes on, his voice a dark, teasing purr. "We're given pictures of all the women guests and their list of what they want done to them."

Of course. I mean, I filled out the questionnaire when I booked, so I should have guessed there was a system behind it. But somehow, it hadn't crossed my mind that the staff would have studied my answers so thoroughly. They know. They *really* know. My throat tightens, and I swallow hard, suddenly unsure what to say.

He kisses the other side of my neck. "As soon as you walked into the grotto, I already knew you were Mandy—the fucktoy slut who wants to be used by every man she can possibly take."

Hearing him say it out loud sends a zing of pleasure straight to my clit. Miguel's voice is hypnotic, sinking under my skin. "You want to stop thinking all the time. Let's see if we can help with that."

He guides me toward one of the alcoves and pushes me down onto the cushion. The space is big enough for several people to share, and I lie back.

"Sometimes the body needs to overwhelm the mind." Miguel kneels in front of me and prods my legs open.

His breath is hot against my inner thigh, and I can already feel the wetness pooling between my legs. He doesn't tease or build up slowly—he dives right in, his tongue flat and firm as it drags over my clit.

"Fuck," I gasp, my body jolting upward.

He holds my hips firmly. "Stay still," he orders, his voice muffled. "You're not going anywhere until I say so."

The other men join me in the alcove, their hands roaming over me. Ben cups my breast and plays with my nipple, while another hand, rougher and more insistent, grips my jaw and turns my face towards him.

"Look at me," Chris demands. "I want to see your face when you come."

Miguel's tongue works my pussy relentlessly, and each lick is a jolt of pleasure. I'm quickly coiling tighter and tighter. Ben pinches my nipples, rolling them between his fingers until my breasts feel heavy and full. Chris's grip on my jaw tightens, his thumb brushing over my bottom lip.

"You like being watched, don't you?" Chris murmurs. "You're on camera and the entire resort could be watching this right now."

My breath is ragged and I can't answer. It's true. Even though it was a fantasy of mine, I didn't even know how much I'd enjoy knowing that someone other than Daniel might watch me. The cameras transform this private moment into a performance, and I'm the star. My body responds to the invisible audience, growing wetter, more sensitive with each passing second.

For a brief moment, as Miguel's tongue works me over, the constant commentary in my head falters before the familiar voice returns.

Gasp and show your pleasure. Make him know you like it.

He flicks his tongue faster, his hands sliding under my ass to lift me closer to his mouth. When he sucks on my swollen bundle of nerves, I detonate. I cry out as ecstasy makes my entire body undulate. Miguel doesn't let up, and he licks me through the cascade of bliss. Ben's fingers tighten on my nipples, sending a sharp burst of pain that only intensifies the delight.

When my orgasm finally subsides, I'm panting and limp. Miguel sits back with a smug grin, his lips glistening. Oh yeah, he knows he did a good job.

If someone had asked me a week ago if I thought the guys would go down on the women here, I would have said it was doubtful. But in my post-orgasmic haze it's crystal clear that this weekend might be about using the women, but it's really all about our pleasure. Every woman should spend a weekend here–hell, multiple weekends. This is my new favorite vacation destination.

"We're not done with you yet." Chris's tone leaves no room for doubt.

He releases my jaw and shoves his shorts down, then covers me with his weight, pinning me. My breath catches as he pushes his knee between my thighs, opening them wider. His thick cock probes my entrance, and my desperation builds.

Oh god, I want this—*need* this.

When he drives into me, I gasp. He feels impossibly thick–maybe thicker than anyone I've fucked before. My moan bounces off the grotto walls, loud and shameless, as he fucks me with furious intensity. Each thrust sends a jolt of wild pleasure through me, rattling my bones, scrambling my thoughts until there's nothing left but the feeling of him pounding deep inside me.

"Do you like my cock?" he grunts. "Do you like knowing your husband is listening to you moan like a little slut for someone else?"

"Yes," I confess breathlessly, my cheeks flushing with arousal. I cling to his shoulders as he takes what he wants. The sound of flesh meeting flesh fills the air, punctuated by his harsh breaths and my continual moans.

"Fuck yes," he hisses, his pace quickening. "Take every fucking inch."

I frantically meet every thrust. When he rocks against a particularly good spot, I whimper, "Please."

"Please what? You want to come? Earn it."

I wrap my legs around his thighs and close my eyes as he pummels into me. He's fucking me so hard, I feel like a rag doll being tossed around. I'm writhing and I cling to him as I'm lost in a sea of bliss.

"Come for me, you filthy little slut."

I convulse as ecstasy short circuits my brain. My mind goes completely blank. No direction, no analysis—just pure, raw pleasure flooding my body. Then awareness returns and he's filling me with his warm seed.

Before I can even process what's happening, I'm rolled onto my stomach. Ben moves behind me, and then I feel him slide his cock deep inside my pussy. Pleasure surges through me, drowning out the voice in my head once again, and for a few heavenly moments, I exist only in my body.

"There she goes," Miguel hums approvingly. "Our mindless fucktoy."

The truth of his words jolts me, snapping me back to awareness—but the pull of that freedom, of being nothing but sensation, is too strong to resist. It tempts me, lures me back toward that perfect, empty state.

Another orgasm crashes into me like a freight train, tearing a scream from my throat.

"Fuck, fuck, fuck," Ben chants, and he drills into me a few more times before roaring as he unloads, adding his cum into my already well-lubricated pussy.

He rolls off me and I moan softly as I'm flipped over again. Miguel is standing next to me, jerking off. I giggle as three shots of cum hit my stomach. He strokes himself, milking out every drop and I move my fingers down to lazily swirl the cum around on my skin.

For a moment, the four of us are quiet. I'm completely happy and sated. It's crazy how an orgasm can quiet my mind.

Miguel breaks the silence first, and his voice is soft and teasing. "You're a mess."

"Mmm hmm, but so good," I giggle.

Chris hands me a cold bottle of water from somewhere. The service at this resort is wonderful. I could come here whenever I needed to unwind.

"Are you going to be okay?" Chris asks, and I know someone would stay with me if I wanted them to.

"I'm fine. I'm going to rest for a minute."

They leave me to recover, and I sit in the alcove, sipping water, processing what just happened. The breakthrough moments when my mind went silent replay in my memory—precious seconds of only physical existence.

I hear footsteps and Daniel is walking towards me. "I saw every filthy moment."

He sits next to me and kisses me. When we break apart, I sigh, "I'm glad."

"You were so beautiful, baby."

His praise warms me, and I yawn. "I think your beautiful slut needs a nap already."

"Yeah," he kisses my temple. "My baby needs to be ready for the Roman Bacchanal tonight."

I might not have been able to fully let go while the guys fucked me in the grotto, but I can tell I'm getting closer to complete surrender. Maybe if something wild happens at the party, I finally can.

Daniel helps me to my feet. "Let's go take a nap together. I'm not going to fuck you again until later tonight."

His statement makes me giggle as I slip my dress back on. If he wants to deny himself the pleasure, I won't stop him. Plus, I might be too tired unless he just ruts away while I sleep. My pussy briefly tries to stir alive at the thought.

Yep, I'm still a slut.

CHAPTER 5

The gossamer toga they've provided for tonight's Bacchanal barely qualifies as clothing. The white fabric is so sheer the pink areolas of my nipples are visible. I don't want anything to stop a cock from sliding into me, so I don't wear panties beneath the thin fabric.

I braided my blonde hair into a crown, the tight plaits keeping the strands off my neck, though I can feel the occasional loose tendril brushing my shoulder. I've paired the toga with flat sandals that I can remove easily. For once, I don't check my reflection before we leave. There's no need—tonight isn't about how I look, it's about how I feel.

Daniel entwines his arm with mine and we follow a torch-lit path to the courtyard being used for the event. When we get there, I'm impressed—flowing white drapes create the illusion of intimacy, with lounging areas surrounding a central space.

In the middle of the courtyard, a raised platform holds a woman stretched out for all to see. She writhes beneath two men, her moans echoing through the night air. I can't look away—the arch of her back, the way her fingers clutch the marble as pleasure overtakes her.

There's a sharp, insistent throb between my legs. I can almost feel the hard stone beneath my own skin, the intensity of being the center of everyone's attention as dozens of strangers watch the men fuck me. I've never admitted it to anyone, not even Daniel, but being observed has always been a feature in my deepest fantasies.

I want that.

The possibility fills me with a desperation I can't shake. I want to be the one shamelessly sprawled out while every eye in the courtyard watches. I want to feel the exhilaration of being on display. Desire threatens to consume me, and I can barely keep my feet from moving toward the platform.

The woman moans again. She's on her hands and knees now as a guy fucks her ass. A bolt of arousal shoots straight to my core, and my hand instinctively goes to my wrist. No green band. I wore the pink and black again, thinking it would be enough. But now—now I want more.

"That's where I want to be," I whisper, nodding toward the slab.

Daniel's fingers tighten around my arm. "I'd love to see you up there. I wonder how they choose the woman."

Sophia appears beside us. "That honor is reserved for our most adventurous guests." She gestures toward it. "Would you like to take a turn there when she's finished?"

"Yes." The word pops out without hesitation.

"Perfect. Enjoy yourself, and I'll come find you when it's time."

As she glides away, Daniel kisses my forehead. "Someone is feeling brave tonight."

I give him a smile as I take in the scene around us. A woman kneels before three men near a fountain, sucking their cocks in turns while her partner watches. Another couple has abandoned their clothing, and he's fucking her against a pillar while her legs are wrapped around him.

I don't know why I want to be in the center of everything. Fantasizing about it and actually doing it are very different things. I enjoy the attention of being the boss at work, but I didn't know it would translate to wanting people to watch me getting railed in multiple holes.

A swell of lust and determination drifts over me. "It's just something I need to do."

I'm already imagining myself up there and my analytical mind kicks into high gear, planning how I'll move and perform.

Daniel pulls me into his arms. "You're thinking too much."

"Maybe." I don't want him to question me too much, so I try to distract him. "Hey, does this seem like an orgy to you?"

He looks around and snorts. "Yes, except none of the men are playing together."

Oh, he has a good point. I read in the brochure that they have other monthly freeuse weekends for various desires. I bet some of them get crazy...though having a platform for a woman to be ravished upon isn't exactly tame.

The screams of pleasure from the woman as she's getting fucked in the ass make me whisper to Daniel, "I wish I'd worn the green band."

Daniel laughs, slipping his hand under his toga. I know he's wearing shorts beneath it since he didn't want to free-ball it.

"You mean this?" He holds up the green wristband.

My eyes widen. "You brought it?"

"Yep, just in case my slut wanted it in all her holes."

Okay, yeah, he's the best husband ever. I pull the black and pink bands off and exchange the green one with him.

He gives me a sly grin. "Now you're truly free to do whatever you want."

The weight of the band feels like permission to surrender completely. This is what I want—what I *need*. And now, nothing's holding me back... well, except for one thing. I could really use a drink. Being a slut is thirsty work.

I tug Daniel over to the refreshment table, and admire the marble surface as we approach. The male bartender smiles as I pick up a glass of grape juice. The tart sweetness slides down my throat while Daniel chats with the bartender.

A firm hand lands on my shoulder, making me gasp in surprise and drawing Daniel's attention. I glance over my shoulder—it's Miguel from earlier. He guides me forward until I'm against the table. I quickly set the glass down, and the bartender whisks it away without a word, as if this happens all the time.

Before I know it, I'm bent over—just a dirty plaything for him to use. My gaze drops to the marble beneath me, the veins in the stone swirling like my scattered thoughts. I clutch the edge of the table as Miguel yanks my toga up to my waist.

"I didn't get to use your pussy and I regretted it," he says as an explanation, and I rest my head on the marble as his hard length slides inside me.

The pleasure makes me gasp, and I clench around him instinctively. He immediately sets a steady rhythm, each thrust shoving me forward slightly. The fabric of my toga is so thin that my nipples brush the cool marble as he fucks me. Sparks of pleasure ripple through me as the delight builds in my core.

I surrender fully to the feeling of being used. I might never have this experience again, and I want to savor it. Each thrust hits a magical spot deep inside me, a pleasure that grows and grows but never quite gets me there.

When Miguel speeds up his thrusts, I know he's close. He finishes with a low groan, his body shuddering. When he pulls out, I straighten up slowly, a trickle of cum trailing down my inner thigh. Holy fuck, this is dirty. Ugh, and I was so damn close to coming.

He straightens his clothes and smiles at me. "Thanks for the second chance."

I barely get out a, "You're welcome," before he turns and heads off.

Daniel kisses my forehead. "You okay?"

"Yeah," I say, though the word feels inadequate. I'm more than okay. I'm restless, eager, and thrumming with unspent energy. "I'm ready for my turn on the platform."

He hugs me tightly. When his hard cock brushes against my stomach, I can't resist rubbing him through his toga and shorts.

"Behave." He grabs both my wrists, pulling them up and holding them between us.

Sophia materializes beside us again. "Mandy, they're ready for you."

Oooh, it's showtime. My heart races as Daniel takes my hand. Each step toward the marble slab feels momentous, and desire simmers in my veins. I've never had sex in front of an audience before this weekend, and doing something this public seems like jumping into the deep end. But I'm ready for it.

"Just relax and enjoy," Sophia says as we reach the platform. "Daniel, you can watch from here." She indicates a cushioned area right next to where I'll be. It's practically within arm's reach with an unobstructed view. "And these gentlemen have expressed interest in joining you."

Five men stand nearby—all attractive, all clearly aroused beneath their togas. I recognize Tyler and Justin from the pool earlier. The others are new faces, new bodies.

I kick off my sandals and the marble is cool beneath my bare feet as I climb the steps. Without prompting, I untie the knot at my shoulder, letting my toga fall to the ground. I'm naked now except for the green wristband, and I lie back on the stone.

Stomach in. Arch your back just enough. Legs at the most flattering angle.

The first man approaches, naked. He kneels between my legs without a word, spreading my thighs wider. I look toward Daniel and blow him a kiss. He's already got his hand beneath his toga and I can see it moving as he strokes himself. Dang, he's not wasting any time. I get a little zing of lust from knowing he's going to touch himself while these men use me.

The man's mouth latches onto my pussy and I moan in surprise. He licks me like he's starving, alternating between giving his attention to my pussy and then twirling his tongue around my clit. He works me into a frenzy, and I lift my hips to meet his mouth, my body already begging for more. This guy is a master at oral. He knows exactly what he's doing, with the way he sucks my clit between his lips and teases me with his tongue.

"Fuck, you're dripping," he growls. "Such a dirty little slut for us, aren't you?"

I moan in response as another man kneels near my head. His cock is inches from my lips, and I open wide. He slides inside my mouth, and I savor the salty taste of his precum. He's rock hard, the veins pulsing beneath my tongue as I lick the sensitive underside. His cock twitches in response, and he grips the sides of my head to control the rhythm.

"That's it, fucktoy," he rasps. "Show me how much you love sucking cock."

I do enjoy sucking cock. There's nothing more powerful than making a guy come with my mouth. I relax my throat and my lips stretch around his girth. He groans, and I hollow my cheeks, sucking harder as he steadily thrusts into my throat.

The man between my legs redoubles his efforts, plunging his tongue deep while his fingers spread my pussy lips wide. Air sweeps over my slick folds, making me shiver. His thumb finds my clit, circling it in slow, relentless strokes, and sparks of pleasure ripple through me.

"Fuck, you taste good." His breath is a warm puff against my wet flesh.

His tongue fucks me with long strokes. I can feel every flick, every greedy suck as he devours me. The wet sounds of my sucking and the man's tongue lapping at my pussy are loud enough that Daniel can probably hear them—a symphony of filth.

Keep your neck at this angle. Use your hand like this. Make eye contact—men love that.

My internal director continues as Justin begins caressing my breasts and pulling on my nipples. Tyler strokes himself, waiting his turn.

"Look at you," Tyler murmurs. "Still a good little fuck-toy."

I'm performing well—I know I am. Their groans and praise confirm it. But I'm still *performing*.

The man between my legs stands and pushes my knees toward my chest. As I'm folded up like this, he has total control over depth and speed. He slides inside me and when he bottoms out, stars pop on the edge of my vision. I moan around the cock in my mouth and I feel a mental shift. Suddenly, I'm not thinking about every move. I'm feeling–experiencing–just being in the moment.

"Fuck, you feel so good," the guy in my pussy grunts as he hammers into me. "Such an eager little slut."

I can't say anything since my mouth is full, but when the guy fucking my pussy groans loudly, I feel his warm cum coating my insides. How many loads of cum is this now since breakfast? Three in my pussy–four? How many in my mouth? I don't even know.

The men trade places. Now Tyler fills my mouth while Justin fucks my pussy. A third guy takes over playing with my breasts, pinching and pulling hard enough to make me whimper.

"You like that, don't you?" he says, twisting my nipple. "You're a little pain slut."

Oh, fuck. I think I might be. The other men surround me. The sensations are overwhelming now. Rough hands roll me over, force me onto my hands and knees. A thick cock slides into my pussy from behind. Another probes my mouth, demanding entry. I open wide, taking it deep into my throat. Hands grip my waist, my hair, my breasts—every part of me. This is exactly what I wanted, what I craved.

"Look at you," one of them growls. "Fucked and filled like the dirty little slut you are."

A hard thrust makes me cry out, and I realize I'm not in control here. I really am their fucktoy. My pleasure builds, drowning out everything but the need to be used. I imagine Daniel watching and stroking himself. I want him to enjoy seeing me like this, completely at their mercy.

"Spread her ass," another voice demands, and cold lube drips between my cheeks. A finger circles my tight hole, bearing down, stretching me. I gasp as I adjust to the feeling of a finger in my ass, and the cock in my mouth explodes. I swallow all I can, but when he pulls out, saliva mixed with cum drips down my chin.

"Relax, slut. You're going to take my cock in your ass while they fuck your pussy and mouth."

The finger withdraws, and for the briefest moment, I'm left achingly empty—every hole wanting, desperate. I don't even have time to mourn the loss before the man playing with my ass stands on the platform and I feel him crouching over me.

The blunt head of his cock presses against my tight rim, inching in slowly, stretching me wider with every breath. *Oh god.* I brace for the burn, tensing on instinct, as I clench around him. I force myself to relax, to open. *Take it. You can take it.*

And I do.

My muscles give way, surrendering to the slow, steady invasion, and heat floods through me. Before I can even settle into the stretch, the other cock drives back into my pussy, harder this time. The dual onslaught steals my breath, sends my mind spinning.

Then there's another cock at my lips, and I don't hesitate—I open eagerly, hungry for more, for *everything*. I suck him deep, my tongue swirling greedily around the thick head, as my body is used front and back.

"Nothing like a tight ass," the man behind me groans. "Feel that, slut? That's all your holes filled."

I can't respond–the bliss is beyond anything I've ever felt. My world narrows to the fullness, and the pleasure borders on pain. The courtyard buzzes with low voices as strangers watch. I imagine them greedily tracking every thrust. I've never felt more free. More present. More myself.

I force myself to look, needing to witness their attention. Dozens of faces stare back—some with parted lips, others with flushed cheeks. A woman whispers to her partner while pointing at me, and knowing that I'm the subject of their conversation makes my pussy clench around the cock inside me. I've spent my life performing at work, but never like this, never so exposed.

And in that moment, I come undone. The climax is a massive explosion, and ecstasy consumes me from the inside out. I twitch with such force that the guys have to shift their positions to keep fucking me.

The pleasure is never ending as I scream around the cock in my mouth. The men fuck me through the bliss and when one guy fills one of my holes with cum, another guy immediately replaces him.

Time loses meaning. Men come and go. I'm moved around, filled again, used in ways I've only fantasized about. Fingers grip my hair, my breasts, and my nipples while I revel in every nasty thing they do to me. Cocks fill my mouth, my pussy, my ass, pounding me, using me until I'm a sweat-slicked, trembling mess.

At some point, I'm aware of Daniel approaching. The knowledge that he's been watching everything—seeing his wife become a spectacle for strangers—intensifies every moment.

He strokes my face tenderly. "You're my gorgeous, filthy slut."

Then he's gone, returning to his seat, leaving me with these strangers who still want to fill me with their cum. And I take it all, my mind blank, my soul alive.

I lose count of the number of times I come, and I don't know how many men use me. It doesn't matter.

When the final wave of pleasure crashes through me, I give in completely. My body arches off the slab, and a sound I don't recognize tears from my throat. Nothing exists beyond this moment.

There is only sensation.

Only surrender.

Later—minutes or hours, I can't tell—Daniel helps me get down. I'm covered in drying cum and more drips out of me.

"You're so beautiful," he whispers as he wraps my toga around me, not bothering to adjust it properly.

When my legs shake and it's difficult to take a step, he picks me up. I wrap my arms around him, boneless and sated.

As Daniel holds me, I realize what I've discovered extends beyond sex. That voice in my head has controlled every aspect of my life. The freedom I found in those moments of silence is something I can take back with me, and truly experience life rather than just direct it.

But first, this slut needs her husband's cock inside her. "Take me to our room and fuck me."

CHAPTER 6

Daniel carries me inside the villa, kicking the door shut behind us. His mouth finds mine in a hungry, desperate kiss. I cling to him, my fingers digging into the muscles of his shoulders. He tastes like grape juice and desire, and I can't get enough.

"Mandy," he moans against my lips. "Watching you tonight—"

"Mmm, I was your good slut."

"You were."

He carries me to bed and sets me down, pulling off my hastily-wrapped toga before laying me back. Then he's sliding my thighs open, exposing my pussy.

"You were so fucking sexy. The way you'd moan and whimper as they fucked you."

My heartbeat kicks into overdrive at the memories of being completely, utterly used.

"I need you," I whisper. "Just you."

He sinks to his knees in front of me, and his breath is warm as he leans in. He doesn't touch me with his mouth, but instead, he stares at my pussy.

"God," he murmurs, and I swear I hear awe in his voice. "You're absolutely drenched."

I squirm under his scrutiny from a mix of embarrassment and arousal. "Because of you. Because you watched me."

His fingers trace the seam of my pussy, teasing me with his feather-light touch. "I can't believe how much cum you took. It's fucking incredible."

He slides one finger inside me, then another, moving slowly. The wetness makes obscene sounds as he finger fucks me, his gaze never leaving my pussy. Holy fuck, this is dirty.

"Daniel," I moan, desperate for more.

He curls his fingers inside me, finding that spot that makes my vision blur. The room fills with the sounds of my ragged breaths as the pleasure builds with each thrust of his fingers.

"Come for me," he commands. "Let me see it."

I come hard, convulsing as my pussy grips his fingers. Wetness coats his hand as he strokes me through my orgasm. When I'm a trembling mess beneath him, he finally pulls his hand away.

"Now it's my turn."

All I can do is lie there and welcome him into my arms. Within moments he's naked and thrusting into me. He's crazed as he jackhammers my sodden pussy.

"Fuck, you feel so good," he moans. Knowing I'm full of so much cum sends a zing of delight through me.

He sets a punishing pace, driving into me again and again. The bed creaks and the sound of our bodies slapping together echoes through the room.

There's another orgasm building as my husband turns feral and growls, "This pussy belongs to me."

His fingers dig into my hips and each thrust is brutal, claiming, as if he's trying to fuck the memory of every other cock out of me.

"Say it," he groans. "Tell me who you belong to."

"You," I gasp, my body quivering with the force of his thrusts. "I belong to you."

He's relentless, and he snarls, "That's right. This pussy is mine. Always has been. Always will be."

Holy fuck, who is this man? This is incredible. I can barely breathe, I'm overwhelmed by the sheer magnitude of his need to own me.

"You're my little slut, aren't you? My fucktoy. My dirty little wife."

I moan, "Yes, your dirty wife."

His cock swells inside me, his veins dragging against my sensitive inner walls. "You love being used. Love being filled with cum, over and over again."

"Yes, yes, yes!" I cry out, my nails clawing at his back. "Love it. Need it."

He suddenly slows down and fucks me with long, slow thrusts. "You're a greedy little thing, aren't you? Can't get enough cock. Can't get enough cum."

My muscles tighten with every filthy word. "Please," I beg, though I don't know what I'm asking for. More of him. More of this. More of everything.

"You want to come again, don't you? Want to come all over my cock like the good little slut you are."

"Yes," I whimper and try to meet him thrust for thrust. "Make me come. Please, make me come."

He slides his hand between us, and rubs my clit exactly how he knows I like it. I'm trembling and my toes curl as he speeds up his thrusts again.

"It's time for my fucktoy to come."

He slams into me and I squeal as my climax obliterates everything from my mind. My vision goes white, the world reduced to the swirling pleasure between my legs. I scream his name, my pussy clamping down on his cock.

"Fuck yes," he roars, his body tensing above me. He slams into me one last time, burying himself deep. The heat of his cum fills me, mixing with the others', claiming me completely. Each spurt of his cum creates a shockwave of pleasure, and I shake with the force of it.

When he's done unloading, we collapse together, our bodies slick with sweat and trembling with exertion. He keeps his cock buried inside me, as if he can't bear to let me go.

"Mine," he murmurs. "You're mine, Mandy. Always."

"Always," I whisper back, basking in the warmth of his possession, and knowing that just as much as I'm his, he's also mine.

He rolls off me, but his arm stays locked around my waist, pulling me tight against him. His heat surrounds me, and my mind wanders, already imagining the way I'll tell my friends about this place. No one will believe me unless they come and see it for themselves.

But that's for tomorrow. Tomorrow, I'll tell the world.

I think back to the deal he made me yesterday—promising to make up for every orgasm I felt I missed on this trip. He's probably feeling pretty smug right now, assuming he's off the hook.

Maybe I'll let him think that.

Or maybe I'll wake him up in the morning with his cock in my mouth and remind him, properly, that he still owes me. And I expect him to pay up. *Hard.*

As I drift toward sleep in Daniel's arms, I realize I've found what I truly came here for—not just the thrill of being used by strangers, but those perfect moments when the constant voice in my head finally went quiet. For the first time ever, I'm simply *being.*

What an amazing journey.

The End

ABOUT LACEY CROSS

Lacey Cross is a wife sharing erotica writer with over 100 short stories published since she started in 2021. Her stories emphasize the pleasure found from the wife living her best slut life and embracing the hotwife lifestyle. She explores themes of free use, submissive wives with dominant bulls, BDSM...and oh-so-many men.